Fucking is Beautiful

Sexy Erotic Stories for Adults Illustrated with Hentai Pictures

_____

Emily White

TABLE OF CONTENTS

INTRODUCTION

Welcome to a captivating journey where my enthralling stories seamlessly intertwine with enchanting illustrations that redefine the very essence of desire in the world of hentai erotica.

Within the secret pages of these forbidden tales, I invite you to immerse yourself in a fiery universe of unrestrained passion. Every word is a whispered moan, and each illustration is a visual embrace that transforms the realms of fantasy into tangible reality.

This collection is not for the faint of heart. It's a bold manifesto, an invitation urging you to delve into the dark depths of lust, where pleasure is painted with audacious strokes and details that promise to quicken the rhythm of your heart. The illustrations are provocative gateways, guiding you into sensual dimensions where every hidden desire finds its expression without remorse.

Are you ready to plunge into a whirlwind of seduction and temptation, where the pages themselves transform into a stage for your most secret fantasies? Allow yourself to be carried away into a realm where sin transforms into art, and art seamlessly merges harmoniously with the ecstasy of desire.

Lift the cover and prepare for an experience ignited by the flame of passion. This is not just another collection; it's your exclusive ticket to the boldest manifestations of anime eros, written masterfully by me, **Emily White**.

FUCKING IS BEAUTIFUL

She had started as an assistant six months earlier and it was winter. She was a little Indian girl who had been adopted, she was very beautiful, incredibly feminine and very wild. I had her in my department and she was very frustrated. She knew that men were attracted to her beauty and everyone looked at her. She wasn't rude but she was distant. In the spring she was worse, not that she dressed poorly, but she dressed like a businesswoman with a fashionable toilet.

She was well built, she had long legs and a nice little ass that could be seen through her panties when she wore white pants or when she bent over, her belly was tanned and she had a superb pair of small but firm tits. She was single but all the men in the company were married, and it was June and we had a little office party. It was June and we had a little office party. Everyone was happy and not thinking about the daily worries and little intrigues that were not lacking as in any office.

It was eleven o'clock and I was heading to the buffet to have a drink. Suddenly he appeared wearing black pants and boots and a blouse that would have turned the heads of most of the men present at this pleasant meeting between colleagues. I was alone and busy drinking a whiskey when I felt someone tapping me on the shoulder. "Hi Johan," I turned around and saw that she was smiling at me, I recovered from my emotions and everything went black. I heard her say later "Johan, Johan, Johan, help me put him in the car" "We are here now" come now, no we can't, it's not far, sit here or lie here.

When I woke up everything seemed strange, I wasn't hungover, I was cold and wondering where I could be, then I saw the bathroom, I took a shower and soon after I felt a little better, I turned off the faucet and took the towel to dry myself.

I had just dried off when she opened the door. She looked up shyly and said, "Well, you slept well, my little piggy," and walked into the bathroom, dropping her robe. She stood in front of me all tanned and completely naked, I was speechless and couldn't help but look at her from head to toe, I admired her beautiful face, her neck, her lovely loving tits whose tips reminded me of juicy raspberries stood proudly and lower down her flat belly and between her legs her little shaved pussy. She was adorable. "Sir, I understand your excitement at seeing me naked," she said, giving me a beautiful smile.

Then I noticed that my long, thick cock was standing in front of me and she was ready to give him pleasure. She took two steps towards me, knelt down and grabbed the cock she wanted with her right hand. She looked at me smiling and soon her pink tongue reached the tip of my cock, from which a few drops of my love liquor were already oozing, which she licked greedily, opened her mouth and nibbled on the glans while her tongue licked in small circles around the edge of my cock. I then pushed my cock down into her mouth to the back of her throat. I let out a moan of happiness and kissed her on the head.

She was an excellent blowjob who had received half of my cock. She started nodding her head and gently weighing my balls and tickling her pussy with her left hand. It was a beautiful sight to see my thick, glistening cock in and out of her mouth as she ran her warm pink tongue around my glans. It was an exquisite caress. Suddenly she stopped, looked at me and asked me to unload in her mouth. "Squirt your sperm in my mouth, dump all your "love" in my throat, I want to taste your sperm and swallow it".

With his tongue he was now licking at length my balls, which he had already massaged with his fairy hands as he gave me this firework I will never forget. "I've never seen a cock that big," she said softly and I couldn't hold back any longer. Then her lips tenderly slid over my glans again and she began to nod faster and faster, she was very pretty, so with a groan I put my hands on her head and fucked her mouth wildly but not for long, I shoved my cock into her deep throat and discharged for many seconds a powerful explosion of cum that filled her mouth, then her throat and finally she greedily swallowed the juicy love liquor with gusto.

I don't think she was prepared to swallow all that cum, because she coughed, sobbed and pulled back as the last spurt of cum filled her little pink mouth and drops of white liquor ran down her cheek. Coughing she scooped up the last drops of cum still oozing from my flaccid cock and swallowed them timidly. "Was it good?" she asked. I couldn't imagine her saying, "It was incredibly good. She stood up and with lustful eyes began kissing me passionately so I could taste my cum, I lifted her up and sat her on the sink.

She was very light and probably weighed no more than 100 pounds. I gave her little kisses on her bottom lip and kissed the soft skin under her neck to reach her beautiful round, firm tits. I started licking and sometimes nibbling on her nipples and massaged them lovingly with my hand. She moaned and was aroused and whispered, "Lick me." I continued to lick her tanned belly, she opened her beautiful legs and showed me her small black shaved pussy. Her pubes were dripping with her wetness.

I bent down and with my tongue all around opened the wet black lips of her swollen pussy. My mouth was full of her juices after slowly licking her pussy lips, she moaned softly in pleasure. My face was wet, she cried out in pleasure as I pushed two fingers into her cunt to make her cum faster, it felt like my fingers were trapped in a vice. I slowly ran my finger up her cunt, while sucking and licking her clit, as much as I could. Then she cried out in delight and I could feel her pussy squeeze my finger. She gasped and laughed as she looked at me lovingly.

I stood up and our mouths met for a long passionate kiss and she took my hand and led me to her room, climbed onto her bed and had her back to me and I had the opportunity to admire her tanned body, it was very beautiful. She was in great shape and I knew she went to the gym three times a week in the evenings. Her ass was beautiful, it was the most beautiful ass in the world to me. I couldn't help but say, 'You are really beautiful.' She replied with a burst of laughter, "I can see you love my body, my body and my ass." I looked down at my cock and saw that it was stiff and hard and was brushing against her belly.... She leaned over and looked me in the eyes and I dreamed of her pretty tanned ass with the pretty black star shaped rosette and the little soggy pussy. Her pussy lips were opening more and more and her little rosette was glistening with moisture. She spread her ass and invited me to make love, "Come fuck me, I'd like to taste your big cock." I couldn't help but place a loving kiss on her little ass.

She moaned when my mouth and tongue landed on her ass. She could feel her pussy was on fire as I licked her delicious little carnation with gusto. I licked the flesh between her pussy and her ass, my tongue grazed her asshole again, and then I pressed my tongue to her secret orifice, in fact I buggered her with my tongue. I licked all around the closed little hole and noticed that she was aroused because she started jerking her finger and moaning. I kept running my tongue over the little hole in her ass, then I increased the pressure on the love hole and saw that her hole opened up and I could push my tongue in.

I thought she was going to cum because she was moaning more and more and jerking frantically and saying, "This is good, really good." I couldn't take it anymore, I stood there with my cock ready to penetrate her. I grabbed her by the hips and laid her on the floor. "Yes, take me, fuck me" she said as she pushed her beautiful ass against me. "With my right hand I grabbed my big cock, bigger than her wrist to be exact and aimed it at her clit. Fuck me now" she moaned and pressed her tight pussy against my huge cock. I held her tight by the hips and began to push my cock in slowly, it was exciting to see her pussy expand under the pressure of my cock, which was filling her completely.

"Careful, your cock is too big, pull it out a little." I pulled out a little of my long 30cm cock and was as excited as a troll. I didn't want to hurt her of course, so I started to slowly push my cock into her cunt and as soon as she moaned I withdrew completely and then resumed my "work" by gently inserting myself again into that channel that was maybe too tight for me. Actually my cock wasn't that big after all, but the girl I was riding was so small, so fragile, so frail that the cock she was receiving deep in her little pussy was to her as big as an electric pole and ... Slowly but surely I managed to sink deep into the target. I had dilated her pussy to the extreme and was satisfied with a job well done, as she cried out her pleasure at being well filled now.

I felt her hand rest on my belly inviting me to stop my back and forth movements because it felt so good to her to feel every inch of my cock being squeezed, pampered and massaged by her beautiful cunt. I stayed still and my cock was clenched in her pretty little ass, I let her fingers slide down her beautiful legs. She started to rotate with her lower belly and I gave her small strokes of my cock. She said, "Fuck me now. I continued to fuck her very slowly giving her little jerks and she seemed to enjoy what I was doing to her immensely. Slowly I pulled out most of the length of my cock so that only my glans was left in the cavity, then slowly I went down to the bottom of her pussy. She moaned with happiness. I repeated this slow penetration several times and then the pace increased.

"Fuck me" she said in a weak voice, I didn't know if I had heard right, "I'm sorry, what did you say? She stroked me, she was aroused and looked at me, she blushed a little, her cheeks were all pink and she replied shyly, "I told you to stick your finger in my asshole, fuck me with your finger, what!

I climbed on top of her with my foot-long cock in her cunt and I was in heaven. I leaned forward and put two fingers in her mouth, she licked them so they were well wet with saliva and then I finger fucked her, yes, I carefully pushed my fingers into her soft warm star shaped rosette.

It opened very slowly and I inserted my fingers.... "Oh! Oh!" I wasn't sure if she was in pain or if this treatment made her happy. I told her, "I will continue, I was overexcited. I realized when my fingers were in her ass, how my cock could slide in and out of her nice tight pussy. Mmmh, that was her response. I alternately pushed my finger and cock in and out of her asshole, slowly and carefully at first, then faster and her cries encouraged me to increase the pace....Progressively I pushed my cock into her pussy and at the same time my finger into her ass with force.

Her wetness flowed over me with every stroke of my cock and also on her leg, it was wet and extremely tight and I could feel my cock inside her with my finger.

I grabbed her side with my right hand and pulled her towards me as I pushed my cock into her cunt. She was screaming, faster, faster, fuck me faster. I started to fuck her very fast and wildly to give her intense pleasure. For this I was in and out of her little black cunt for many minutes and she was screaming with joy, I could feel in my cock that her orgasm was near and she felt gasps in her cunt that started to wet my cock with my cum, as her rosette opened and closed to the rhythm of my strokes and if her cunt was tight, her ass was even tighter, her asshole felt awfully good and she screamed that it hurt when my cock made contact with her ass and she gasped with excitement. She knew how to use her ass to take my cock deep into her bowels, two big strokes of my cock got the better of that too tight hole and my hot cum flowed for endless seconds into her bowels. I had finally fucked her and it felt so good to get my cock out of that long tunnel.

She was beautiful even when she was on her knees with her ass in the air and her tanned, sweaty skin glistened adorably. Her asshole was torn and red from the harsh treatment I had given her. My whitish cum dripped from her shithole down the reddened lips of her cunt and spilled onto the mattress. It was a sight I would never forget. I had never experienced a fuck like this. She woke up, a minute ago now, she lay on her side and looked at me like she was a strange person, I laid down and picked her up, stroked her hair, her chin and held her close to me, I had never thought she was there, I was exhausted. I stood there with her and was happy and satisfied with my skill, but I still felt an emptiness inside me. I fell asleep and the doorbell woke me up and I saw that she was gone. I heard voices of women.

A little later she came back with a hot brunette woman, about 25 years old, probably Arab or Turkish. She said, "Hey, I'm Anna and this is Julia you just saw, she's a good friend of mine. Before I could say a word Julia smiled and said, "She fucked me too. I was wondering what was going on here. But before I could say a word, Julia said, "Look, you can see, I'm sure we both have red assholes" and she dropped her dress on the floor and climbed on the bed, knelt down and bent over to show her girlfriend her asshole. Anna looked at me and Julia's ass and lingered on the pink lips that were quite swollen. She bent down and saw the asshole sticky with cum and the cunt wet, she inserted a finger into the asshole and cunt and brought the finger to her nose, sniffed and realized what had happened. Julia had been fucked and fucked...Julia turned around and approached Anna, "Let me help you take off your clothes. "I don't know," Anna said, "should she watch? 'That's exactly what she's going to do,' said Julia, and began to remove Anna's blouse. Anna had on a white lace bra that was nicely filled with her big tits.

Julia looked at me fondly and unhooked Anna's bra and said, "They really are beautiful breasts, aren't they? Haven't you often had the pleasure of looking at more beautiful ones? Then she buried her face in her friend's soft, warm breasts. Anna's breasts were round and firm and very large, her nipples had a very proper diameter. 'Yes, her breasts are really nice,' I said, looking at Anna. Julia had in comparison to Anna a young man's body. Julia had removed Anna's pants.

Anna stood there naked with her long brown hair partially covering her breasts, she was really beautiful with her long legs, flat stomach and spherical ass. She climbed onto the bed and I had a chance to see her little pussy. Her pussy was shaved with the exception of a small black tuft of pubic hair. Julia firmly said to Anna, "Kneel down so he can see when you lick her.

Anna looked at me with lustful eyes and leaned forward, her round ass was taut and showed off her pussy which was very different from Julia's. Anna's pussy lips were glossy and all red and her rosette was not star shaped. Julia stood behind Anna, stuck out her tongue and licked Anna's asshole as well as her clit and the exquisite black pussy lips. She started ruining her clit with the red tip of her tongue and looked at me.

Julia drank Anna's wetness like a kitten lapping up her milk, her face glistened with wetness and I could see she was biting her bottom lip as both of her tits swayed and rubbed to the rhythm of her movements. Julia sped up." Come help me, do exactly what you did with me" "No," Anna replied, "there is no way I'm going to slap your ass. I got up and crawled over to Anna's wet pussy and plunged my tongue into her slit. Ella felt her pussy was on fire and smelled intoxicating.

I heard Julia say, "Not there," and she grabbed my hair to bring my head down to her ass, "Lick her ass like you did mine. I slid my tongue all the way to the bottom of her rosette slit as Julia continued to lick and suck her clit, "Fuck her with your tongue" Julia asked. Anna tried to lower herself, but received two hard slaps on her ass, "So hold still." Anna moved her ass while I licked her little ring. Gradually she had relaxed after Julia's wedges and I was able to insert my tongue into her asshole.

Suddenly Anna had a very long orgasm and her pleasure was exquisite. Anna's face was flushed and Julia was lovingly kissing her cheeks. I was sitting next to her breathlessly looking at these two beautiful women and my cock was again erect ready to penetrate a mouth, cunt or ass. Julia arched her elbows for a while and smiling looked at my stiff, red cock waiting for her and asked, "Do you want to fuck her?"

"Of course I want to fuck her," I replied. Anna looked up and saw my cock and once again got down on all fours and handed me her delicious little ass, she was all excited and said, "Come and fuck me."

I felt Julia grab my cock and moisten the glans with her saliva saying, "I know what you want, it's Anna so you'll get it today. She pushed my cock against Anna's newly opened sticky red rosette. She moaned when she felt the glans graze her asshole. Julia held Anna's slowly expanding ass and my cock was able to push inch by inch into her tight asshole. Her ass squeezing my cock was a beauty, it was a perfect ass. I pulled my cock out of her ass, her asshole was open and she sighed as I shifted my position to fuck her better from another angle. Standing up I took her by the hips, pulled her to me and she was able to get on all fours on the edge of the bed.

Slowly I pushed my cock into her ass and she could feel her sphincter "marry" my cock beautifully. Julia was beside me stroking my ass and whispering in my ear, "She likes to be fucked hard." So I increased the pace and gave her big strokes with my cock. Anna moaned and said, "Faster, faster, harder, harder." I pressed firmly on her hips and pounded her with all my strength, my cock went in and out of her ass with lightning speed and my balls slammed wildly against her cunt. Julia squatted down and licked her pussy and alternately inserted a finger into that delicious shaft.

I was lucky enough to have already discharged twice, so I could easily hold back even though the girl was good. Anna started screaming, I was tense and sweaty and Anna kept screaming, "Ah, that's good, that's good, harder, faster". I did everything I could to satisfy her. Suddenly she let out a horrible scream and I could feel that her asshole had adapted wonderfully to my cock to make me cum, after a tasty massage she liked to give me with her ass muscles.

From Anna's pussy a powerful jet of wetness splashed onto Julia's face as she lay underneath her in the "69" position. This very exciting scene encouraged me and I sent several spurts of cum that warmed her ass in a particularly nice way, then I decanted very slowly. Her asshole was torn and very red. I was very proud of the results. Anna felt the opening with her fingers and said tiredly but happily, "I won't be able to sit down tomorrow. I was lying on the floor, when Julia stood up and exclaimed: "I'm beautiful with my face covered with "honey" and stroked Anna on the ass. Anna slid two fingers into Julia's cum stained asshole and began to push them in. Anna gasped.

Anna laughed and exclaimed, "I don't know you well enough," and pushed her fingers in. Ann moaned, groaned but remained on her knees as if she knew what was coming. Julia turned to me and asked, "Give me the tube in the top drawer." I opened it and among the adult toys I found the tube. I handed it to Julia who pressed it right away or it will be tight" and then she was able to push her fingers all the way into her asshole after dipping them back into the lube.

Anna cried out, the pain was so great, and she clung to the sheets as her sphincter tightened against her benefactor's fingers. They lay still for a moment and Julia inserted the fingers of her free hand into Anna's pussy. Anna roared and moaned and although she seemed to be in pain, she was actually experiencing more pleasure than pain. My cock became very stiff again and Julia noticed and said, "Here's another one who is very aroused."

After a while she asked Anna if she was ready. The latter answered in the affirmative with a low moan, Julia slowly began to push her hand deep into Anna's pussy, then did the same alternately in her ass. At first they were only light movements. Anna lay with her mouth open in a trance and moaned to the rhythm of the roaming hand and Anna was very aroused, Julia withdrew her hands a little from the furnace and Anna moaned more as she reintroduced them into both of her love holes.

Julia had changed her pace and removed her sticky hand from Anna's ass. Her asshole was bright red and as the ring slowly closed Julia pushed her hand back in and withdrew her other hand from her pussy only to reintroduce it a few seconds later and speed up the movement. Anna cried out and it was hard to tell if she was enjoying the treatment or in pain. Now it was a hellish rhythm and Anna screamed even louder as she felt Julia's fist in her ass and pussy. Anna's face was flushed and she screamed horribly again and felt strong shocks and several wet sprays came out of her pussy and spilled onto the floor. Julia couldn't help but say, "Now that's a woman who likes to be fucked and be fucked." She wiped her hands on the sheets.

Anna, still on her knees, was petrified and gave me the opportunity to look deep into her gradually closing asshole. Julia had settled on the bed next to Anna. Anna was slowly recovering from her emotions and let her hands gently slide over her belly, which was very sore, while Julia gave her a long kiss on her face.

I'M A BITCH!

I'm a bitch!

Bitch! No, you're not! I'm a well-known lawyer, well-built they say about me, very fuckable according to some frustrated people, not a crush as you can see. I'm not going to make an appeal but to tell you about myself.... At the instigation of... You'll find out later!

How did I become what I am now?

Oh, I don't claim to be a white goose, far from it! My sexual life has been studded, since I was fifteen, with experiences that, though fleeting, have left indelible marks on me.

Thus my older sister, particularly wild and always eager for sex, introduced me to lesbianism. With her domineering temperament, she made me a perfect submissive until I was eighteen. Deciding on our every sexual relationship, my pleasure, etc. All of this with the utmost discretion to our parents, our family and school relations. This is how I learned to mask the truth and to consider that lying could be an elegant way out of trouble.

It allowed me to experience male sex, and I was actually deprived of male sex after I turned eighteen. She was a student I had seduced early in my undergraduate studies. This short-lived relationship led me to discover orgasm with a man, fellatio, in which I very quickly became an expert for all my passing lovers.

Because far from leaving me the choice of my lovers, my sister, increasingly vicious, proposed to many of those who came to fuck her to also fuck the young woman I was. This was appreciated by the boys in question, to fuck both sisters in succession. Somehow I had become my sister's whore.

But the whore I had become always refused to allow these multiple lovers to penetrate her anus. Occasionally I would tolerate the intrusion of dildos, or ball strings, from my sister as long as my arousal was due to long preparation and was at its peak, and in any case they were only small tools.

When I met the man who would become my husband, he was none other than someone who had fucked me as a sister and enjoyed my submission, he became my regular lover before asking me to become his submissive and wife. Because he was tireless in bed, he quickly convinced me. I was addicted to sex, and feeling him pour into me several times in a night was pleasurable; I became a nymphomaniac with him. He exhausted me with repeated orgasms.

Knowing that I was bisexual, since I was available to my sister, he tolerated my escapades with her, promising me more lesbian adventures. Dazzled by these promises, I forgot to protect myself with him and naturally became pregnant.

It was under these conditions that the future doctor became the boyfriend of the future lawyer, because there was no talk of abortion. During this time my sister had married a bank executive and had a daughter. This justified my freedom to fuck as I wished with Yves.

After my studies I became a mother.

Unconsciously my libido wilted and I attributed the decrease in our sexual relations to my husband's respect. In the meantime, he had opened a practice as a general practitioner and was particularly busy, which justified his sexual abstinence. For my part, I had resumed my law studies and was looking forward to the future with confidence. As for my daughter, she was cared for during the day by her grandmother in the company of her cousin.

When I finished my studies and was sworn in as a lawyer, I was almost thirty years old. My father told me that he had played with time to hand over his estate to me. Of course, I had no choice but to accept, with all the difficulties that entailed, since all of his colleagues would be retiring within the next four years. I then became a recruiter of lawyers. In retrospect, I must admit that my recruits were generally women of various ages but pleasant in my eyes. The fact remains that, two years later, there were four women in their 40s and 25s and two men near retirement.

I was busy, my husband was busy, or so I thought, and my daughter was growing up being cared for by her grandparents on Wednesdays in the company of her cousin, whose mother, my sister, led a more than dissolute life as far as I knew. Unfortunately, I was so busy with my own affairs that I responded only briefly to her requests for sisterly moments.

Certainly, I neglected myself, not caring about my appearance, heedless of my femininity as I enjoyed the sometimes affectionate outfits of my co-workers.

It was in this atmosphere that it all came crashing down.

***

For once, I was home early enough. After taking over for our maid and looking after my daughter, I prepared dinner, not without grumbling to myself about my husband's tardiness. When my daughter was in bed, I turned on the TV to pass the time, but I wasn't seriously interested.

Eventually he appeared, looking as concerned as ever, and I couldn't help but scold him for both his tardiness and his frown. Inevitably, without turning up the noise level of our exchange (so as not to wake the girl), he drifted off to more complaining.

We came to blame each other for our respective lack of attention, and I defended myself by claiming that I was responsible for the study and had a low libido. I was then entitled to a retort that I still remember:

- You were more available despite your studies when you were a whore for your sister!

My retort was also acerbic, like:

- And you were more willing to fuck me!

That's when everything changed!

- That's not what other people say!

- What!!! ... Others? Are you cheating on me?

Despite myself, the tone had suddenly risen. A long moment of silence between the two of us followed this question. My thoughts collided, the surprise of this revelation leaving me speechless. I saw my husband's face cross all colors. When he finally broke the silence, he confessed in a voice that was barely audible.

- I've wanted to talk to you about this for a long time, but I never felt it was the right time.... Well, maybe I never had the courage....

I remained silent, baffled by these words. He resumed his confession. Then I realized that he had been sexually dissatisfied since the birth of our daughter and had had many affairs with various patients who were probably as frustrated as he was. But most seriously, he had fallen in love with one of them.

Stunned by these revelations I sat back and let him continue. Then I learned that this woman was none other than a young girl studying at the university. He had met her during a consultation and had been seduced by her maturity, and what's more, she was black, Senegalese to boot, and had come to France to become a business manager, her parents being large landowners in her country.

Sexually he was completely satisfied with this girl, she had no taboos, according to him she enjoyed his cum and besides being fucked like a real whore, she accepted to be sodomized without any problem. What I had always refused!

Finally, the apotheosis.... At the end of the school year, she had to return to her country to take over her parents' business, and Yves had already planned to join her as soon as possible. He had therefore contacted various NGOs to obtain a permanent position in the country in question. Totally devastated by this succession of revelations, I fled to my bedroom without even eating dinner. I quickly undressed and went to bed.

Unable to sleep, I tossed and turned in my bed. I thought long and hard about the situation I was about to find myself in. I had no worries about my financial future, I was making a good living. I was more concerned about my usual living conditions, our maid arriving too late to take my daughter to school, and other similar difficulties I would face.

When I woke up, I realized that I had spent the night alone; Yves had been thoughtful enough to sleep elsewhere. I had, despite the nightmares that plagued my night, made my decision. So I got up and made breakfast. While my daughter was eating breakfast, I called my office to let them know I was going to be late, then I showered and got ready. I took care of the little one and in no time we were ready to leave for school.

That first morning alone went well and I arrived at the clinic only fifteen minutes past my usual time. As soon as I arrived I asked to see Simone.

She was the first woman I had hired, she was divorced and also had a daughter. I told her my situation and asked her to handle my divorce.

My choice was perfect, judging the urgency of the matter, Simone expedited the procedure and was able to reach her whore quickly. So I found myself a bachelor with a family at the end of the school vacations.

You may wonder why I call this girl a whore? Quite simply, because when Simone was researching my case, she discovered that her parents were not only large landowners, but also ran a dozen brothels in various cities around the country. Also, after the settlement meeting with my Ex, and after talking to him about the matter, he told me:

- You can come and work for them if you want to resume your activities as a young whore!

The two years that followed passed quietly. As a free thirty-something, I divided my time between my work, practice was growing, and daily life. My daughter was now ten years old and quite mature, which relieved me of the constraints of motherhood. The only noteworthy change was that I was more available to my family: I saw my older sister more often, who was alone during the week, and my daughter enjoyed spending entire afternoons with her cousin.

One day we were alone, it must have been a Saturday because the girls were out. The conversation turned to sex. My sister said to me:

- You who used to fuck so easily when we were young, don't you miss sex?

This question reminded me of my ex's reflection. I told Anne about the comment....

Anne - He was right, everyone who fucked us praised your fucking skills!

Me - But he was also one of those who took advantage of us!

A - Believe me... You were a good whore to me then, have you lost your gifts?

M - You're exaggerating, I don't feel the need to fuck like you say.

A - I think you really do need it, but you don't want to admit it....

While saying this, Anne had pulled up my skirt and put her hand on my pubes....

A - Besides, you already get wet when people talk to you about sex! See, you're still the good bitch I knew....

The worst part was that the wetness of my underwear proved him right. I tried to control myself, but this hand on such a sensitive and intimate area of my body disturbed me too much to the point that I mechanically spread my thighs to better offer myself to this caress.

A - Well, my dear! I see you are still as sexy as ever. Let's go to a quieter place and there we will be more comfortable to continue....

The words were soft, but the tone had hardened and the memory of my obedient youth came back to me. Once again it was Anne, my teacher and initiator, who returned, as did my submission.

I allowed myself to be pulled into the room and she carefully closed the door, telling me:

- Get naked little sister, just like the good old days.

Docilely I did so, quickly removing my clothes. I remained naked while she did the same, she ended up lying on the bed, raised her knees, spread her thighs, revealing her perfectly groomed pubes and ordered me

Come lick me! I hope you haven't lost your good habit of making me cum with your tongue.... Come on slut!

I didn't respond to these contemptuous words and settled between his open thighs with my face pressed on his lower belly. My tongue immediately inserted itself between her labia majora, searching for her clitoris, which I knew to be very sensitive. During this lingual exploration, my hands had risen from the thin line of hair that remained on her firm breasts that I kneaded without delicacy, so much had I missed this contact for years. The memory of our lesbian embrace came back to me. I found the smell and taste of the powder Anne's belly was not sparing itself with, she was getting wet like a whore (I was no longer the whore)....

I could feel my belly burning. I too had to get as wet as possible, the moisture invading my sex, oozing from my orifice and running down my thighs. Anne's hands pressed my temples. For a few moments, she reached for my hair and pulled me onto her. Our naked bodies were fused together. We shared a long, long kiss. Our tongues sought each other, rolled around each other, caressed each other, our saliva mingled. Finally satiated by this loving contact we stood cheek to cheek, catching our breath. My heart was pounding, so intense had this moment been.

- Rub your breasts against mine....

I obeyed immediately, our arousal-hardened nipples caressing the firm breasts, which warped under their pressure. Our breaths became shorter. Our Venuses were no less, swaying to touch each other better.

Feeling Anne on the brink of pleasure, I straightened up and with my thighs wide open, we began rubbing our sexes together. Clitoris against clitoris the pleasure overwhelmed us at the same time.

Collapsing on the bed we recovered from these wonderful orgasms. Anne broke the near silence, interspersed simply with sighs and breaths.

R - You see, my dear, you need sex....

M - I have to admit that I enjoyed this lesbian embrace.

R - Now that I have you back, I promise we'll do it again!

M - Yes, but I also have obligations and responsibilities... I won't be as available as before....

A - Of course, Lise... I understand... Let's have a nice shower before the girls come back.... Then I'll have some proposals for you...

* * *

Quick shower, we soaped each other up without too many bold gestures.

Rinsed, dressed and made up, we went back to the living room. To relax, I made tea and, curious, took the initiative to start the conversation again.

Me - So what do you have to offer me?

Anne - What we just did together shows that you are sexually unsatisfied. Am I wrong?

M - Without a doubt! I admit I enjoyed those moments, it reminded me of our youth.

R - You see that you missed it. But at that time you were submissive to me, you fucked my lovers on my orders, you accepted all my requests, moreover I noticed that you obeyed all my requests just now.

M - Yes, of course it came back to me quite naturally.

A - Are you still willing to be my whore?

I don't know why, but probably the memory of what we had just done, I replied.

M - Yes, I will obey you as before, you can do whatever you want with me.

R - Very well, Lise. (Yes, that's my name) You know my husband is away all week, and since I can't go a whole week without fucking, I found a solution. There is a very nice swingers club after N..... where I can get laid discreetly, without the risk of running into someone I know. The owner and her waitress are also very nice and bi, which doesn't hurt. I'm sure they'll like you, beautiful as you are.

M - Are you going to prostitute me too?

A - No my dear, but since the club is only open at the end of the week, I'm only free on Thursday nights. But since I'm quite close with Tamara, the owner, she often invites me on Monday or Tuesday nights to private parties.

M - What's your point, Anne?

A - Simply that you come with me at first to get to know me and then if you like you can go alone.... I'll take you next Thursday. I'll take you next Thursday, okay?

I looked at my journal before responding. I didn't feel like I had any binding commitments for Thursday afternoon and Friday.

M - Okay, Anne, but I will have to find a babysitter for my daughter.

A - No problem, you'll sleep over at my house, my parents will be happy to watch both of you. But you'll have to change your look a little bit....

M - What does that mean?

A - No hair, I want you smooth all over, especially your sex. No fancy hairstyles, you won't be able to retrieve your clips and bobby pins. Simple clothes to take off, skirt and sweater, short or very short skirt and tight or sheer top. Most importantly no bra, and preferably a thong at the bottom....

M - Do you want me to look like a whore?

A - Somewhere, yes! But for free, you can fuck whoever you want or I'll tell you. You know, there's a certain respect for women in this kind of place, otherwise you'll be expelled and forbidden to come back.... By the way, wear self-fixing stockings or a garter belt with stockings.

M - Well, so many recommendations....

A - Yes, I want Tamara to find you to her liking.

M - Will I have to seduce her?

R - No, it's usually the other way around. But believe me, she is a perfect lover....

M - I can already feel my pussy wet, with all your stories!

R - I suspected your libido needed stimulation, I'm glad this afternoon helped you. I promise you can have all the cock you want in my company. I wondered how the little slut that you were could become such a chaste wife?

M - I must admit that my business has not left me much time to think about sex!

R - Precisely, it's urgent at your age (I was thirty-four at the time) to think about taking your own pleasure and enjoying life

M - Stop it, Anne! You're making me too wet, I'll have to change my panties again!

The girls' return interrupted this scabrous conversation. While they were enjoying their cokes. We worked out the material conditions of the evening and then Anne decided that they should go home.

The four days that followed would have been nothing extraordinary had I not constantly had this evening in mind, which according to my sister promised to awaken my libido forever.

Every moment I detailed my collaborators, telling myself: what would you think of me if you knew what I was about to do? I tried to gauge their seductive power. To judge their clothes, alas rarely provocative, putting myself in the shoes of a pimp, I wondered about their ability to bring me back. I also dreamed of establishing a classification among them....

Thursday morning I went to my hairdresser and in the afternoon I went to the beauty salon I had booked for a "full" waxing. The young woman who greeted me was the one who was to take care of me. She immediately put me at ease by offering me a coffee to relax. The room was furnished only with a gynecological chair covered by a thin mattress. While she prepared the instruments and ingredients, I undressed completely, then naked and a little anxious about her reaction, I lay down in the chair. The mattress was very comfortable, she turned to me and put a towel on my lower belly, saying in a very soft voice:

- So covered you will not be embarrassed by your nakedness.

With a smile of thanks, I raised my arms to reveal my armpits, which were not very hairy but needed to be perfected. She was as gentle as her voice as she worked, stroking me with a soothing, scented lotion after removing the wax strips. Then came the inspection and smoothing of my legs, as carefully as ever.

In the meantime we exchanged platitudes, about the weather, about body care, etc. He complimented me on my beauty, on how my breasts held up, on how successful I must have been with men and women, claiming that I must have provoked their jealousy.... In spite of myself, under these compliments, with what I imagined to be my evening, I felt my groin moisten. I was ashamed of my weakness and felt the air on my lower abdomen as she removed the towel and whispered in my ear:

- Don't worry, I'm a lesbian! That's why I've been entrusted with the full books, I won't hurt you....

Then she began to cut my hair with a scissor, spreading my thighs as wide as possible while putting my feet in the stirrups. For a moment, I had the impression that my pubes were as hot as the hot wax he was spreading, all this sexual tension disappeared when he withdrew it, making me cry out in pain, quickly calmed by the caresses of lotion.

At her request I lay on my stomach and with my buttocks spread open by me, I offered her my anus which she undertook to meticulously rid of all unnecessary hairs. Not being a fan of sodomy I judged this question unnecessary. Having made this observation to her, she replied:

- It is normal to be perfectly smooth in all places, it also allows all orifices to be flawless and easy to maintain.

I told myself that her lesbian tendencies must have been at the origin of this observation and at her request I inspected my pubes. Surprised, I was perfectly smooth and this nudity mechanically incited me to release my clit from her hood. Seeing my gesture she threw me:

She - Don't do that! You excite me too much!

Me - Why?

And - I want you too much! I told you that you are very beautiful, I mean it....

As she turned to hide her dismay, I realized how much I had disturbed this young woman and quickly put my clothes back on. It wasn't until I left the room and went to the cashier that I learned the young woman's name was Sarah. At the checkout counter the woman who was supposed to be the owner of the establishment remarked that I was a new customer. And it was a great surprise. For a long time, too long for my liking, she repeated this. Fortunately, the final caresses were enough to overcome the pain, even triggering spasms of pleasure.... Am I satisfied with the service?

Me - Of course, Sarah was wonderful! I'll be back with pleasure...

Sarah - Thank you, ma'am. I too will be happy to take care of your beautiful body.

With this exchange of compliments, I couldn't help but draw Sarah close to me and kissing her on the corner of her lips, I said:

- See you then...

I ended the afternoon by buying some ultra thin black micro-net thongs that I learned, and several pairs of hold-ups, in silk, polyamide and mesh, with and without seams. I planned to let Anne choose the stockings.

Searching my closets, I found a straight black miniskirt with a slight side slit and a T-shirt that I considered too small but now did nothing to hide the shape of my breasts and nipples, which when they hardened stretched the fabric indecently.

To hide this libertine attire, so as not to shock my daughter and the neighborhood by going out dressed like this, I planned to put on my rather stiff mackintosh. To my surprise, my daughter came home from school and found me young and very pretty. This day, full of compliments about me, had made me very excited. So, as soon as dinner was over, I went to take my daughter to Anne's and learned that we were waiting for her.

I learned that we were waiting for a friend who would accompany us. She was a good friend of Anne's that she had originally met at the club. She was a lesbian and her partner was a police commissioner, unfortunately not very forthcoming. As a result, Katia often went with Anne to indulge her lesbian fantasies and to find new models because she was a photographer and worked for foreign websites. Thus Anne appeared more often nude on these sites. And this frequentation, of Katia not the sites, had introduced her to many depraved women like herself....

Katia is a beautiful blonde, twenty-five years old, quite tall, with long hair, hazel eyes and a delicious mouth topped by a small nose. I liked this girl right away and it worked at first. She was sweet, smart, confident and I told her about my beauty salon discovery. She asked me for the address to feed her client sites. Anne and Katia validated my outfit and chose the fishnet stockings.

During the trip, Katia, seeking confidences, told me about her business. About her very varied models, from young to mother, sometimes both together, lesbians or not, whores and women of the world.... Of the places where she poses, her studio, the models' houses, the countryside, the sea or the river, especially the very classy relay held by a lesbian friend... It was a real lecture on her art. Of course, she proposed me to pose for her, and also my environment, my family and my collaborators....

Between my natural curiosity and her propensity to talk about herself, we didn't see any time passing and we arrived. I was about to discover this place of debauchery where I was going to have the time of my life. The girls ordered me to leave my mackintosh in the car. Timidly I followed my mentors towards the entrance of this place of perdition.

LAURETTE

- Okay, let's take a closer look. Michel, please lie down on the exam table.

The doctor takes a seat at a monitor's desk next to the bed. As she walks around her desk, her blouse hangs down for a second, revealing the tanned skin of a bare thigh. Catching my interested gaze, she smiles and restores the order of her dress.

- Your husband's eye is always so mischievous!

- I know, I've given up on changing it," agrees my wife Francine.

What's wrong with that? There's no shame in enjoying a pleasant view.

- 'What do you want, at my age you can't change it,' I replied, heading for the consultation table.

I like Laurette, whom I met as a young doctor when we first moved to the area. Since then, she and her husband Georges have become our friends, well to be honest, especially my wife Francine's. This is quite understandable given the age difference. I'm within a year or two of my wife's age, who has not yet reached fifty, while last year I was forced into an unwanted retirement, prompted by a board of directors anxious not to keep a manager past 65. Oh, it wasn't because of petty material considerations that I delayed my departure date as long as possible; my retirement is comfortable, thank you. I didn't like spending my days alone in the apartment while Francine worked as a department head at the prefecture.

Well, that's all in the past now and I have to admit that I don't miss the hectic professional life. I can now devote myself to my wife, whom I used to neglect because of my professional concerns. What a pleasure it is to go out together without having to worry about putting on a good face the next day at a meeting with staff representatives or at a reception for a very important client or to show the factory to a regional or even national celebrity or to resolve a conflict between two directors! We rediscovered a real life of a couple and Francine's good humor is a pleasure to watch.

...Done, because for a while now, I think I've been dragging my feet too much. Francine became concerned about my tired appearance and, taking the pretext of what I hope is a passing faint, dragged me forcefully into Laurette's office.

- Take off your pants," she ordered in a professional tone.... "Your pants too... More than that... Come on, Michel! Don't be a fool! How do you want me to examine you!

I push the bottom halfway up the thigh.

- Ah well!

He manipulates my bag. How soft his hand is! Francine stares at me wryly. I wipe the smirk off my face and look away. Laurette taps the soft penis resting on my thigh. The reaction is immediate: the thing gets bigger and longer.

- Well, nothing wrong so far, says the satisfied doctor. We'll check your prostate.

He moves an ultrasound detector over my lower abdomen and carefully observes the patterns on the screen.

- Um, um... Well, I'll do a rectal exam. He lifts his pelvis.

She puts on a latex glove. Laurette, her face expressionless, rotates her finger. Oh, that feeling! I control with difficulty a sigh, there is no way Francine is laughing at me! Another sigh as the finger leaves her anus. The examination could have taken longer!

- What's wrong with him? What's wrong with him?" asks my wife.

- The prostate is a little big, but that's almost normal at his age. All we have to do is look at him.

Laurette hands me a piece of paper to clean up the gel she used for the ultrasound and tosses it along with the glove into a basket. She pulls her chair closer to the exam table and lifts the penis with the back of her finger. The penis remains soft despite the gentle rubbing.

- However, I find his sex a bit sluggish.

- I'm worried too," adds Francine, who stands up and takes my hand.

The two women look smugly at my scattered family jewels. I feel ridiculous and curse my lack of reaction.

- Do you think if you pet it...? suggests Laurette.

- I think so, she usually loves it.

- Do you mind?

Without waiting for an answer that she knows is affirmative, the doctor manipulates the soft shaft with two fingers. I am terribly embarrassed. A hand other than my own or my wife's is caressing me. This has never happened to me since our marriage. Laurette slides the sensitive skin under Francine's interested gaze. The swelling of my penis betrays the pleasure I feel. I am ashamed and angry with myself for not being able to control my reflexes.

- Oh, stop!" exclaims my wife.

- Yes," adds Laurette, "it almost offended me!

- Fortunately, she got over it.

Since Francine tolerates another woman touching me, I stop feeling guilty. Do they want to fondle me? I have nothing against that! Laurette manipulates me. Her palm closes over my dilated shaft and the caress turns into a full-blown masturbation. I don't know what that means therapeutically, but I'm no longer ashamed of my newfound virility and surrender to the gentleness of the treatment.

- Can you help me, Francine?" asks the doctor.

- Yes, how?

I smile at my wife who puts an eager hand forward.

- 'As soon as he reaches maximum rigidity,' Laurette explains, 'you'll hold him while I check with....

- Arrgghh!

A few drops splash out of the meatus and land on the doctor's wrist and Francine's hand.

- Oh, the pig! You couldn't hold back!

- Uh...I'm sorry but I couldn't. It got away from me.

- It's just like home," my wife adds, gently drying me off.

Laurette takes my sex in her hand. A few flicks of the wrist to no avail. She absent-mindedly plays with the soft shaft. It does me a world of good, though without any physical manifestation.

- Well, no need to insist," she says, abandoning me. You can put your clothes back on.

The loss of her fingers on my penis makes me sigh.

- Um... is that all you do for checks?

- Please, Laurette," Francine implores, "I'd like to know where I stand.

- Fine, I accept. Help me restore his manhood.

I am thrilled. Two beautiful women all to myself taking care of my sex! I close my eyes, not wanting to know who is doing the testicle rolling and who is the doctor or my wife. Despite the closeness of ejaculation I feel my penis swell and stretch.

- Aaah!

A mouth closes over the glans. I open my eyelids to see Francine, her eyes rippling with restrained laughter, sucking my cock between her lips. Wow! I can't believe it! My wife performing oral sex in public!

- Let me control the stiffness, Laurette pushes her.... No, it's no good, she declares, pressing down on the bending bar.

She handles the rod, alternately covering and uncovering the glans.

- No, it's not over yet... Allow me.

Laurette leans over and swallows my sex. This is conscientiousness! Oh this tongue! As soft as Francine's! This is the first time I've heard of a fireman as preparation for a medical checkup. Maybe modern medicine?

- Arrgghh!

Once again my body is out of control. The ejaculation comes without warning. Surprised, Laurette swallows some of the semen and spits the excess into a handkerchief. She's about to burst, but changes her mind at my sheepish expression.

- You really do have an erection problem," she says when we return to her office. You're ejaculating without achieving the rigidity necessary for penetration.

- Can't you prescribe some Viagra?

- Um... Laurette once told me that it's not worth dreaming about.

- I told you that?... Um... You're right, Michel," he confirms after checking his computer. It would be incompatible with the treatment for your heart.

- What can we do?

- Um... Male problems are very difficult to solve. Known treatments are restrictive and success is not guaranteed. I will think about it and consult with some fellow specialists. I will contact you as soon as possible.

Laurette writes a prescription. Francine fidgets in her chair.

- If I understand correctly, the gentleman's goliathing is over, at least for the time being.

- You couldn't say it better yourself," smiles Laurette.

- And what about me? Where do I fit into all this?

I look away so as not to meet her furious gaze.

- What do you want me to say?" says Laurette helplessly. Do you want me to prescribe a lover for you?

- Oh, aren't you ashamed?

I add my grain of salt.

- I can see the pharmacist's face from here.

- Or maybe a cure for winter sports? Preferably without your husband.

- It would be the same thing, I can't help but add.

- You. You better shut up," Francine says.

She puts her bag away.

- Calm down," consoles Laurette. I promise I'll get back to you as soon as I can, and hopefully with good news.

- I thank you.

We embrace like old friends as if the erotic interlude, a first between us, were a parenthesis without consequences. On the street, Francine has regained her good humor.

- Don't worry, honey. In a few days it will be over.

I'd like to be as confident as she is....

In the evening, in our bed, Francine snuggles lovingly against me. We exchange a long kiss. We are used to being naked. Nothing interferes with our mutual caresses. I know she loves to feel my hands roaming over her body as a prelude to the act of love. She purrs in pleasure as my fingers and tongue explore her secret nooks and crannies. His hand slides between our bodies to my lower abdomen, his fingers encircling my sex.... My penis, swollen with desire, cannot stiffen. Francine is stubborn.

- I can do this!

She sinks under the sheets.

- Aaah!

A warm mouth takes hold of the glans. A tongue passes over it, titrating the meatus. I feel the shaft expand, stretch and harden.

- I knew I would succeed!

Francine, proud of the result, stands up. Without leaving her trophy, she squats on my belly, directs the cock between her thighs.... Unfortunately, the penis bends instead of penetrating. Worse, I can't resist the sudden surge of desire and I spill over the edge of the much desired vagina. I am desperate.

- My dear, my dear, forgive me, forgive me. I am no longer good for anything.

Francine hugs me and cuddles me.

- It's nothing, my darling, it's nothing. I was presumptuous to believe that a simple visit to Laurette would be enough to cure you. We have to be patient.

- You... You think so?

- I'm sure of it.

We embrace for several minutes, then I gently pull away.

- My dear, allow me to make you come with my caresses as I am not allowed to do it otherwise.

She smiles at me and gets on my back. I sink under the sheets.

- No, not like that. I want to caress you at the same time.

- How can I tell her I'm dreaming this?

How can I tell her I'm dreaming it but that I won't be able to physically show her the pleasure she'll give me?

- Don't you want to? Does Laurette have to be there?

- Don't talk nonsense.

- What is it? What are you waiting for to get into position?

I step out from under the sheet to go back, but in the opposite direction, with my head between her open thighs. I sigh in relief as her fairy fingers fiddle with my wrinkled penis and a delicate tongue caresses my testicles. I push aside the hairs of her sex to reveal her secret little knob, which I unlock.

- Yes!... Aaah!

I work my way through the folds of flesh that are moistened with the dew of pleasure. With my fingernail I tickle the entrance to her vagina, penetrating the length of a phalanx.

- Aaah!

Her mouth encircles the flaccid cock that serves as my sex with warm saliva.

- Arrhh!

- Hey! Don't forget to stroke me!

- All... Aah!... Now.

I insert two fingers into the love pit and one into the secret hole behind. His tongue rolls my glans against the roof of my mouth. What a sensation! Never before has an oral caress given me so much pleasure. Maybe because of the flexibility of my cock, which is unusual at these times? I nibble on her clit. Francine shudders. My sex, which she has swallowed almost completely, muffles her moans. I feel her close to orgasm and I activate my caresses.... There... Yes! My fingers lap at her dripping vagina. Suddenly she closes her thighs imprisoning my head. Ouch, she almost bit me. No big deal.

After a few seconds Francine removes my cock from her mouth.

- I'm sorry, I can't accommodate you.

- Yes, you can! Go ahead!

- But it doesn't seem to have any effect on you.

- You'd think it would, but I assure you it's delicious.

- Oh, it is! Well, since you say so

She takes her lollipop again, unconvinced. I grunt with satisfaction and try to appease her intimate lips.

- Ah well! It took me a while, but I did it!

Francine is proud to feel the shaft growing between her lips and activates her licks on the shaft. I'm both disappointed and happy. I'm happy to regain a manhood that had eluded me, but a little disappointed that I can no longer feel the glans roll under my tongue in a delicious caress. The world is a bad place! Too bad, it's not Francine's fault and I try to give her another orgasm.... Ouch! The sap rises in the stem. No, not yet, it's too soon!

- Stop it!... Please!... Arrrgh!

It's too late! Before Francine realizes she has to stop sucking, cum flows into her mouth. She dutifully swallows and finishes cleaning her glans while my fingers run over her orifices and my tongue scrapes her clit.

- Aaah!... Yes!

I disengage and move to her side, holding her close to me. Her breathing calms down.

- Forgive me my dear, I took too long. Next time I promise I'll be careful.

- You are a treasure.

Three days later, Laurette calls me. She makes me an appointment with a well-known professor. This time it's a man. His brusque manners don't do me any good, nor do those of his assistant, a surly nurse who seems to have a fierce hatred for men, judging by the nasty looks she gives me. After several tests and checkups, this specialist gives me little hope. According to him, my corpora cavernosa are in poor condition and I will not, unless a miracle happens, regain the rigidity necessary for introduction. I am devastated, oh! Not for me, but for my wife. Although Francine assures me that the mutual caresses we exchange under the comforter are sufficient for her happiness, I know there will come a time when her body will require more substantial sexual nourishment.

How difficult it is to grow old...

***

It has been three months since my erectile dysfunction was revealed. It has been three months since I have been able to make love to my wife of 20 years younger, even though I am past retirement age. We have learned to compensate, the caresses we exchange in bed at night meet my low expectations, but from her growing nervousness, I see that the same is not true for Francine. She misses penetration, this is a fact even if she won't admit it to herself. I need to find a solution. Who do I turn to? Allow her to have a lover? My subconscious matchmaking is reluctant. I agree to let her have a functioning cock since it is necessary for her balance - our balance - but I don't want to be left out. I accept the idea of her taking pleasure in the arms, not the arms, of another man's penis as long as I am present and participate in her enjoyment. Yes, that's fine, but how do you do it? Search the internet? No way! I'm too afraid to meet scammers.

The more time passes, the more urgent it is to find a way out. I'm convinced that a lover would be the least worst solution when I bump into a former colleague while walking around town.

Over drinks, we exchange memories. I ask him about life at the company where I was one of the top executives. The discussion turns to the marital problems of this or that colleague and he confides to me, under the seal of secrecy, that he has solved his marital problems by joining a swingers club with his wife. The information clicks in my brain. Could this be the solution to my problem? Without sounding pushy I get the address of the club. He even offered to sponsor me. At the next meeting he gave me an invitation card, which was essential to get into the place. So, after two long weeks of struggling to get Francine's consent, we showed up at the door of the club one Friday night.

I check the invitation card for the address of the building in front of which my wife and I are standing. As I go to ring the doorbell, Francine holds my arm.

- Do you think we're doing the right thing?

- We've discussed this. You agreed that this is the best way to deal with my disability.

Francine sighs.

- I don't want to put you through this.

- I just want you to be happy.

I press the doorbell... In response to my knock, a window opens. I hold the box in my hand. After a few seconds, the door opens and the guard invites us in. He leads us to the locker rooms, one for each gender. There I find my colleague greeting me. He asks me to write on a name tag the name I want to introduce myself by. My first name, Michel, will do. Francine joins us. As we introduce ourselves, I smile when I see "Laurette" on her name tag. My friend guides us toward the bar and leaves us for a while. I can't resist the pleasure of teasing my wife.

- Oh, hi Laurette, what a surprise to run into you here!

Francine blushes.

- I didn't dare give my first name as you.

- It's not serious, I don't think our friend is here.

- You know, I'm ashamed.

- Of what, darling? For borrowing your name? There's no reason to be.

- It's not that. They asked me to take off my panties... I heard it's the custom here.

- Well, well, this is interesting," I say, patting her butt.

In fact, I can see her bare skin under the thin fabric of her dress.

- You're not going to leave me, are you?

I didn't want to, but I'm so proud of her for asking.

- I'll stay by your side, I promise.

My friend joins us on the arm of a very young girl. With a mischievous smile, she lets me know that my wife is not the kind of woman she is looking for in this place. I prefer it. As we talk, a man about Francine's age, maybe a little younger, approaches her. His nametag says "Joseph." I answer him with a smile. My wife, after a quick glance, turns her back on him. She doesn't say anything but I feel her cringe. I continue the conversation with my friend and his companion, trying not to lose sight of the man.

Is this a good number? Will he accept my presence? Will he be able to satisfy my wife? Where will it happen? All questions without answers.

Suddenly Francine is startled and abruptly withdraws her hand.

- Oh!

I look closer. A long, stiff sex points through the open fly. The man looks at us a little surprised by my wife's reaction. Our friend interjects.

- Please excuse Mademoiselle Laurette. This is her first visit. We must give her time to absorb the atmosphere.

- I apologize for my boldness, I will wait for Mademoiselle's signal," he says, stepping back and gathering his paraphernalia.

I think he'll have to wait a long time because I doubt Francine will call him back. We finish our drink. I think my friend is eager to take his conquest to a quieter place. I assure him that everything is fine and that we can do this. He leaves us relieved.

But Francine panics when he leaves. The glass shakes in her hand. I pull it out, fearing an accident, and she snuggles into me.

- Kiss me!

Her tongue meets mine and begins a voluptuous dance in my mouth. Out of the corner of my eye, I notice that Joseph is getting closer. He's right up against Francine, she has to feel him on her back.... Yes! She stops every movement not knowing what to do.

- Is the young lady reassured now?

No answer. Francine hides her face in my neck, her ear against my mouth. The young man moves behind her. He lets out a small cry and presses himself against me. I am consumed with curiosity.

- What is he doing?

- He...he's lifting up my dress.... Kiss me!

I take hold of his lips. It's my turn to explore his mouth. Francine accepts the game. Joseph understands her well and pulls up the fabric. I can't see very well but I'm sure his hands are on my wife's butt.

- What is he doing to you? Tell me what he's doing to you...please.

- He... is caressing my buttocks.

- Do you like that?

- Or... Yes, yes... You're not angry with me?

- I love you.

I kiss her on the neck. She gasps.

- Oh, God!

- Is it me doing this to you?

- No, it's her hand...between my thighs.... Aah!

- Is she stroking the sex?

- Yes... Mmmh!

My decision is made in an instant. I unzip my fly, take his hand, and slip it into my pants.

- Caress me, my darling.

His fingers wrestle with my underwear, reach my shaft and squeeze it.

- Tell me, what is he doing? Caressing you?

- Yes... Oh! His fingers...

- What are his fingers doing?

- They... go inside... Mmmh!

His fingers move my sex and torture it. I don't care, I'm too excited.

- Oh! They go away... No, they come back... But... Ooh!

- What's the matter?

- They're not fingers, they're...

Joseph leans over behind Francine. I think he's positioning his cock.

- Oooh! He enters... Aaah!

The tremor that shakes Francine during his introduction is transmitted from his hand to my sex. I am overwhelmed. Joseph begins the love dance.

- Is he a good fucker?

- Shut... Shut up!

He masturbates me to the rhythm set by Joseph. I look around. No one seems to notice us, maybe this situation is common around here. I help Francine to stand up on her legs. Her hand gives me an immense feeling of well-being. What a joy to rediscover the feeling of a hardened penis and resist the rush of pleasure. This hasn't happened to me in months! And it's nothing compared to the pleasure of feeling Francine vibrate as she did in the early days of our marriage.

- Aaah! I...I loved you," she stammers.

She brings her foot into my arms, my wife. The man waving behind her doesn't count. We are both alone in the world locked in our own bubble of pleasure....

But everything has an end. Joseph is getting more and more aroused. He speeds up, sighs louder and then releases his pressure in a long moan that Francine accompanies. At the same time I unload into the fingers that caress me.

It takes almost a minute to fall back to earth. Joseph pulls out, tosses the condom into a nearby bin, and packs up his gear after cleaning his glistening cock. Francine folds her dress and leaves us for a quick ablution after placing a light kiss on my lips. She has managed to contain my seed in her palm and I can safely zipper up my fly.

I am relieved. This first experience is a success. I can already imagine doing it again. Next time we strip, to add epidermal contact to our pleasure, but Francine won't agree to do it in public, even though naked couples move around the room without embarrassment. She needs more privacy. Are there discreet spots in the club? I'll have to ask my friend.

My wife joins us, beaming. I congratulate myself once again on the success of my plan. I feel that we have found the solution to our problem. Joseph accepts the drink I offer him. He suggests that we get to know each other better at his home where my wife would be more comfortable than in public.

- It seemed to me that she would rather not make a spectacle of herself.

This matches my thoughts so well that I have no objection.

- What do you think, my dear?

Francine is more doubtful. I must insist that she agrees. Joseph leaves us for a moment.

- I'll be back in a few seconds. He orders one last drink on my tab, we'll leave the club when we're done.

Francine refuses to let us into Joseph's car. It would have been better for me because I've had a lot to drink and I'm tired. Nevertheless, I manage to follow him without a problem and park my car in front of his building. We follow him into the garage and go up to the apartment.

I am surprised to see him close the door behind us. An exclamation from Francine makes me turn around. Two hilarious individuals are standing in front of us. I realize I've been remiss. We need to get out of here and fast!

- Is this what you call privacy? Open the door immediately!

- You're in no position to dictate your terms, fatso," Joseph replies, raising his hand to me.

This is not good for him. I have some notions of close combat. I grab his arm and twist it violently.

- Aooouh!

- Come on! Open the door or I'll break your arm! Stay by my side, my darling, we're leaving....

A brutal pain in the head and then nothing....

I open my eyelids. Joseph, bending over me, wakes me up with several slaps.

- Ouch!

- You see Laurette, you shouldn't have worried, your man has a hard head.

I want to get up, but I can't, my hands are cuffed to the uprights. My hands are cuffed to the bedpost where I lie naked as a worm. With a groan, I turn my face away. On the next bed, Francine lies handcuffed and naked, a gag over her mouth. Terror is in her eyes. What a fool I was to lead us into this trap! I am furious!

- Stupid...

- Shut up!

Whack! A masterful slap shakes me.

- One more word and I'll gag you like your charming companion who didn't realize there was no point in shouting. Isn't that right, my darling? Do you want me to remove your gag? You won't scream anymore?

Francine shakes her head in denial. Joseph reaches over and removes the sticky plastic.

- Ouch!

Joseph releases her hands and she hastily massages her sore lips.

- Well, I think our guests are calming down. We can begin the festivities. First, let me introduce you to Bill....

A tall, blond man bows.

- ...And Jules.

This one, a short-haired brown man, giggles stupidly.

- And this is Laurette, who will do her best to please us," Joseph continues, proud of his role as master of ceremonies, "and ... Excuse me, my dear, I forgot the name on your badge. Can you please help me? There's nothing more disappointing than being addressed by periphrases like, "Hey there, come here bitch" or "Move your ass, bitch." So what's your blazon?

- Erm... They call me Michael.

- Very good, Michel. Imagine, friends, that Michel, here, has taken the young lady to a select club, whose name I will not mention for the sake of discretion, for the sole purpose of watching her fuck... What's going on, Michel?

His irony hurts me even more because it hits the nail on the head.

- You're in luck because I promise you'll get a lot of eyeballs.... Don't you agree? I don't understand you. There are three of us taking care of her and you're not happy? What else do you need?... Hey, stay there!

He grabs Francine who was getting up.

- Uh...I'm going to the bathroom.

- All right, I admit it. Go with her, Bill, and don't take forever.

Despite the dire situation, I can't help but admire Francine's perfect figure, which would be the envy of many young women under 30. My jailers agree with me, judging by their mischievous eyes when my wife disappears from their sight. I sigh, it's not to reassure myself!

- Say, Joseph?" asks Jules. What do we do with this?

- I told you, it will watch us at work.

- Don't you think it could be useful?

- What do you mean?

- Well, it also has a mouth and an ass.

- Ah, well, why not? Wait till you're free and you'll have the pleasure of joining in.

He releases one handcuff but stops when it's time to open the other.

- No, that's not wise. It's just that it has hurt me so much before. You'll be tied up by one arm, but I promise that won't stop you from getting off.... Hi! Hi! Hi!

He giggles stupidly, proud of his dubious joke.

- There you are!" he interrupts when Francine and her jailer return. Sit down, my beauty, we've wasted enough time. You get down on all fours on the bed.... What, you refuse to obey?

Whack! A masterful slap shakes my wife who tightens her lips. Angrily I pull at the handcuffs without being able to free myself. Joseph grabs Francine's arm and throws her onto the bed, cuffing her limb.

- On all fours!... Faster than that!... No? At ease! Jules, go get me the hammer!

This comes back with the device. I hadn't seen one of these since I was a kid. I remember the spanking my mother used to give me. It hurt so much!

- Aooouh!" Francine groans under the bite of the straps.

I look at her, sorry for my helplessness. She sighs and climbs into the covers.

- Ah, I see we're getting reasonable," Joseph laughs. Nothing like a little spanking to lighten the mood.... Yes... Get your ass up... Even more... Well, stay like that. And you, Michel, stay like that... Faster than that... Do you want a taste of the whip too?. Okay, we can start.

Joseph pulls down his underpants and underwear to his ankles. He tangles in his clothes as he climbs onto the bed and takes them off.

- I don't need them anyway," he grumbles as he gets behind Francine.

Jules mimics him, laughing. I shudder as I feel his hand spread my thighs and grab my sex from underneath. Under other circumstances I think I'd like that. On the next bed Francine moans.

- No, I don't want to.

- What don't you want? Didn't Joseph's old man make you come just now? Don't you want to do it again? I do!

Joseph spreads Francine's thighs and searches the position of her vagina with his hand.

- Hey, it's ready! We're going to have fun together.

He sharpens his cock with a few flicks of his wrist and pushes in all at once until it comes against her buttocks. Francine moans and arches her elbows to resist the thrust. Jules inserts a finger into my ass.

- Aah! Don't hurt me.

- Relax, fat man.

He spins the finger around. Ooh! That feeling. Suddenly he pulls back.

- I'm not a sadist, I'll lubricate you.

On the next bed Joseph, with many moans, beats my wife who hides her face in the blanket. Jule returns. Something icy enters between my buttocks.

- Hello! It's cold! What is it?

- Never mind! You'll thank me.

The thing (frozen margarine?) is replaced by a warm lump. A firm grip, the sleeve penetrates dilating the anus. Ssssh! How it hurts! I dread to think how much pain I would have felt if my tormentor had pierced me without preparation. I grit my teeth so as not to give him the satisfaction of my pain. "I'm fucked...I'm fucked...some bastard is fucking me...I'm fucked..." these dirty words echo in my brain to the rhythm of the cock pounding my foundation. Why am I thinking right now about young offenders thrown to confirmed criminals in an overcrowded cell? Are they as overwhelmed as I am by the rage of helplessness just as strong, even stronger, than the pain?

- And what happens to me?

Look Bill, the third thief is coming. What else will they invent for our misfortune?

- You'll have to... Han!... Get sucked off... Han!... While you're waiting... Han!... Your turn, Ahane Joseph.

- By whom?

- Your choice.

Bill removes his pants like his colleagues and climbs onto Francine's bed. He wants to present his sex to her mouth but has to give it up because the poor girl is too shaken by Joseph's kidney strokes. He falls back on me. I panic. How can I avoid this further humiliation?

- I...never have.

- All the more reason to start, open your mouth wide and don't make jokes or you'll get hurt.... Knock it off, Jules, just until I get inside.... Here... You can go.

I can barely breathe as the cock fills my palate. My jaws tug from being wide open but I don't dare let go for fear of hurting the glans and unleashing a rage that I fear will affect me and my wife.

Gradually I take the measure of the two introductions, in my ass and between my lips. In the long run it is less unpleasant than I feared. With my tongue I tickle the tip.

- Yes! Go ahead, you suck like a champ!

It's silly but I'm proud of the comment. The friction in my sphincter softens and sends some beneficial waves to my sex. It would be perfect if Jules stroked me at the same time.... Perfect? What am I saying? Francine and I are being raped by three weird guys and I'm talking about perfection! Because of Bill's dick I can't see how it's going on the other bed. My wife is complaining but she doesn't seem to be complaining, which Joseph confirms.

- Be happy... Han!... Michel, look... Han!... How Laurette is coming... Han!... The same with everything ... Han!... On time at the club ... Han!... You can't see ... Han!... It's a shame but... Han!... You can trust me... Han!... On my word.

Behind me Jules accelerates.

- It's too good!... Aaah!... I'm coming!... Arrrgh!

He pushes me with violent loins. Bill, as a precaution, withdraws his sex and I can finally close my mouth. Two more thrusts and Jules collapses on my back. I turn my face away. Francine gives me a smile that turns into a sneer as she orgasms. She throws her ass in front of Joseph's cock, moaning in pleasure with each introduction. Joseph was right when he said I was lucky. Yes, I'm happy for her enjoyment. At least everything isn't negative for her.

Ouch, a cock pushes violently between my buttocks. It must be Bill taking Jules' place. I grit my teeth on my pain. And once again I consider myself lucky because the cum in my sphincter made the introduction easier. Bill is fucking me at a hellish pace. I brace myself on my elbows to resist better. At this rate he won't last long. Next door Joseph and Francine are amplifying their moans. They won't be long either.

- Hey Michel! You don't seem to like what we're doing to you and your wife," Jules says. 'And yet we're putting our hearts and souls into it!

- Um... Yes, yes.

No need to provoke them, I'm in enough pain as it is.

- So why don't you get an erection?

He's having fun manipulating my flexible penis just as Bill is getting loose in my bowels. This is too much. I can't help myself. The sap rises and flows down Jules' fingers.

- The bastard! He jumps on me. Have you seen Joseph? He unloads without an erection!

He wipes himself on my buttocks.

- I see, ahahaa Joseph. He came to do... Han!...his wife at the club.... Han! Han!... You missed my... Han!... My beauty.

- Good thing we're here to make up for it, aren't we Jules," says Bill, getting out of bed.

- Yes! ... I love it!... Aarrgghh!

Joseph screams his pleasure and collapses on top of my breathless wife.

- 'Your Laurette is a first class fucker,' he congratulates me. 'It's a shame you can't enjoy her, but you're in luck, my friends will take care of satisfying her.

- Oh yes, they will! I can't wait to taste this wonder," Jules says.

He approaches Francine, who is lying on her side in the fetal position.

- Here," he says, showing off his cock, "give her the strength back and then I'll show you what I can do.

It hurts me to see my wife take it and bring it to her lips.

- Suck me too," Joseph orders. It's my turn to taste your ass.

He hides the other bed from me. Too bad, I would have liked Francine to see me do what she did. I work on my wife's secretion covered cock....

This went on all night. As soon as our lollipops reached their goal, our torturers penetrated Francine's sex or my ass. They were inexhaustible. Each of them must have taken five or six strokes. My anus is on fire, Francine's pussy probably at the same point. My jaw cramps from spreading my teeth. Finally, full of sex, we're abandoned.

- We'll let you rest for an hour or two," Joseph says, "but don't worry, we'll be back with croissants and friends. We want you to be satisfied with your weekend.

- Oh no! Francine whines as the door closes. I'm not going to stand for this.

We're still on the bed, one arm cuffed.

- I'm keeping you and your swingers club idea.

- Forgive me honey, I know, it's my fault, I should never have agreed to follow that Joseph.

- You don't know what I've been through.

- Uh... Yes, I do. I'm in the same boat.

- Sorry, dear, I forgot.

- You'll soon see that it will all be a bad memory.

- Yes, but if we have to suffer the same treatment all weekend I will not survive.

- No, you won't. We'll get out of here immediately.

- What? Are you a magician? Are you a magician? Abracadabra and open handcuffs?

- No, but hand me the saucer on the nightstand... Yes, that.

I had noticed that Joseph was holding the keys to our handcuffs after locking them on our wrists. How many times I shivered during the night, fearing that our torturer would find a safer place. Francine holds out her arm. Too much running.

- Hold on, I'll move your bed.

Pushing with my feet I manage to slide the bed away. Francine grabs the saucer and tries to insert a key.

- I can't do that.

- Give me the keys.

She hands them to me. Too far away, I manage to pull her bed with my foot. With my fingertips I touch the keys...they're about to slip out.... No! I grab them and manage to free myself then free Francine. We uncover our clothes that haven't suffered too much. My wallet is intact as well as my trousseau. Our torturers were bad men but not thieves. Fortunately, the locks open from the inside. We don't have to force the door to escape. We find our car intact at the foot of the building. I mentally thank Francine who wouldn't lend me our executioner's car. Half an hour later, we relax in a hot bath. Holding her very tightly against me, I calm my wife, who can't stop shaking, against the emotion of deliverance.

I am furious with myself. How could I have been so careless? It was obvious that we shouldn't leave the club, that I shouldn't accept Joseph's sinister invitation. Francine had been more perceptive, I should have listened to her. I hope she's not too angry with me and forgives me.

***

Later that day I phoned Laurette, asking her to come and examine us, insisting that she come to the house instead of receiving us in her office.

The doctor begins with Francine.

- Can you give us a few minutes Michel, I'll call you when I'm done.

- Um...

I am disappointed because I had asked the doctor to come to our home to assist with the exam. I receive unexpected support from Francine.

- She can stay, you know, I don't mind, on the contrary.

- Well, that's up to you.

Is it an illusion or did I detect a hint of spite in Laurette's voice? At her friend's request, Francine lies down on the bed, legs open, offered. She offers me a hand, which I hasten to take. Laurette settles between her open thighs. What is this? She doesn't put on a glove. Gently she spreads the sensitive flesh, explores the entrance to the vagina.

- For the moment I can't see anything serious.

She takes a speculum from her purse and carefully inserts it, eliciting a groan again.

- Ouch!

Her tone worries me.

- What is the problem?

- I've never seen such erosion! What did you take, my dear? It is fortunate that there are no wounds or bleeding.

He puts away his torture device and carefully examines the scarlet vulva. Francine tightens her lips but I can tell by her smile that it's not the pain that makes her sigh.

- The clitoris has not suffered, all the better.

It seems to me that the examination goes on longer than necessary, something Francine doesn't complain about. Would she be sensitive to female caresses? What am I saying here! She is sensitive to caresses and that's all, I know. Whether it's me or Laurette who does it doesn't matter. On the other hand, this surprises me. He seems to take real pleasure in the examination. I didn't know he had this Sapphic inclination. What does it matter? Does he bow, kiss the offered sex? No, our friend stands up with a sigh and gives me a dirty look. This is why he wanted to be alone with Francine! I'm the disruptive element.

- You're doing fine. I'll prescribe you an ointment and in a few days it won't show. Your turn, Michel.

- Should I take my pants off?

- That question! Sure, and your underwear too! Let's go, come on! Hurry up, I don't have all day.

- How can I go on?

- Get on all fours on the bed, ass in the air.

He retaliates by leaving me in a humiliating position while he cleans his speculum. Francine sits on the bed and caresses my cheek. Laurette approaches menacingly with her torture device.

- Well, for both of us... Spread your knees... More than that... Not brilliant.

She strokes her anus with a finger. I sigh as I reach for my ass.

- Hey, hey, he seems to like it.... Good to know," he adds in a barely audible whisper.

- What are you saying?" asks Francine.

- Nothing... Careful Michel, I'm putting the camera.... Does it hurt?

Yes, but I can't be any softer than Francine who underwent the exam without batting an eyelid.

- A little, it's sensitive.

She pushes it in and turns it around, making me wince in pain.

- Be careful Laurette, you're hurting her, my wife intercedes.

- I do it as gently as I can.... Well, they didn't spare you either. Well, there are no deep lesions, it will heal quickly. I'll prescribe a restorative ointment for you too....

Laurette puts her things away.

- Well, children, you're doing well. You won't be left with any side effects.... Erm... I hope they had condoms.

- No!

The doctor jumped up angrily.

- No condom? But you are crazy! We have no idea about such recklessness!

His anger seems disproportionate, we are still the ones who are primarily concerned.

- You know Laurette, they didn't leave us any choice.

- Well, excuse me. You're also due for a blood test in about two months. We'll see you with the results. Take care of yourself in the meantime.

It leaves us here alone with our worries. I hope we didn't catch anything!

Two months later, Laurette calls us into her office.

- I have the results of your blood test.

Francine grabs my arm.

- What's wrong?

- Nothing, everything is normal.

What a relief! Francine and I look at each other, smiling. Another bad memory fades. Laurette seems as happy as we are.

- A good thing, right?

Francine stands up:

- We thank you for this pleasant news, but I must leave you, I must prepare a visit to the office of a high official.

- Please don't go so fast, I would like to examine you again.

- But I am well, I assure you.

- Let me be the judge of that. And you too, Michel, I will examine you at the same time. Take off your clothes.

What is it? Aren't you going to ask me to leave the room? That's good! I would have refused anyway. Francine is the first to lie on her back, torn apart.

- At first glance, nothing strange... When I do this, does it hurt?

- Ooh! No!

- And this!

- Aaah!

What is the reason for this examination? Would he suspect me of sadistic practices on Francine to compensate for my disability? I lean in closer. Laurette's touch is more like the caresses I give

Francine than a medical examination. A finger titrating her clitoris and two others inserted into her vagina make my tender wife sigh. Laurette is aware of my presence. She blushes and straightens up.

- Well, everything is fine, no problem. You can get dressed. Your turn, Michel.

- I don't see why Francine should have a problem. I assure you I'm not doing anything wrong.

- I'm sure you're not," smiled the doctor. 'Do you want to stay, Francine, while I examine your husband, or would you rather go back to your office?

- At this point, I'll stay.

I'll take my turn on the exam table.

- How many times do I have to ask you to remove your underpants and underwear!

A little embarrassed, I find myself in my underwear. I get on my stomach.

- What are you doing in this position? Turn around!

- Uh... I thought you wanted to check out the back.

- I don't!... Hey! Hey! Looks like he's sorry.

- Uh-oh...

- Look at this little, no, this big bad man who wants me to examine his ass. Did you like it that much last time? I want to please you.

- Uh... No, that's not necessary.

Vexed, I turn to the front. Laurette takes in my paraphernalia, first my testicles which she rolls between her fingers, then my penis which she turns easily.

- Hum... No progress at first glance. Isn't it hard? Francine.

The latter, who is staring with a lucid gaze at the hand manipulating my soft shaft, takes a few seconds to react.

- Uh... I'm sorry... No... Uh... Well, yes, from time to time but it doesn't last. Not long enough for penetration.

If Laurette's caress wasn't so pleasant, I'd send these women away for laughing at me!

- Ah, it seems to be getting a result.

- Let me see!... Oh yes, it's getting bigger, you're lucky. Can I touch it?

Francine's fingers replace Laurette's hand. I close my eyes, concentrating on slowing the rise of the sperm. Unfortunately, my efforts are futile and the drops of semen fall on my wife's wrist.

- No improvement, the doctor says. I think you need to take your share, Francine.

- Come on, fatso," he consoles me, "I love you anyway.

That's no consolation. It's urgent that we find a palliative that meets my wife's needs without endangering our marriage. We dress in silence.

- Are you free this Friday? George and I would like to invite you.

After exchanging a glance with Francine, I warmly accept.

- Good, we'll see you at 7pm.

- See you Friday...

After the meal, which was very good, Georges took me into the living room while the women cleared the table and prepared the coffee. He takes out the cups and saucers and puts them on the coffee table. He looks embarrassed, looks at me, opens his mouth and then turns his head.

- Is there anything you want to tell me?

- No...

Strange, I would have thought. He sits down in an armchair and motions for me to follow him.

- Well, yes," he corrects himself. You know, Laurette told me about your problem.

I frown, confused. What did she have to disclose about my problems? What about medical confidentiality?

- For my part," he continues, "I really enjoy your company. I would be sorry if you didn't get along. I wish there was something I could do for you.

What's your point? I let her muddle through her explanations.

- I've always had a soft spot for Francine.... Uh... So Laurette and I... Uh... We thought... Uh... That for her... Uh... I could...

I've got it! She proposes to make up for my failure and fill the role I can't take on for my wife! The nerve of her! Furious, I stand up on my forearms and let myself fall back to the floor. Wouldn't that be the solution? Yes, I'd rather trust my friends not to drive us apart.

- I won't do anything to stop you...if Francine agrees.

- Of course she will.

He looks relieved. Oddly enough, so am I, as if I'd been expecting his proposal. On reflection, it was predictable: an invitation to a party right after the stroking session in Laurette's office.... Obsessed with my own problems, I hadn't noticed it.... My subconscious had figured it out....

Laurette and Francine return from the kitchen. My wife is all red. She comes and sits on the arm of my chair and kisses me near the ear.

- You know what Laurette proposed to me?

No need to specify, our friends shared roles to convince us.

- I get it, George informed me. Is this what you want?

- I... I don't know... I love you, you know.

He turns his misty eyes to me. The idea of making love to George does not deter her, but she hesitates to take the plunge. It is my duty to encourage her.

- This could be the solution for us, my dear," I say, nibbling on her earlobe.

- Let's drink the coffee, it will get cold," says Laurette, filling the cups.

Francine sits on the couch next to her friend. We sip in silence, each of us in our own thoughts. I can imagine our friends are wondering if their project will succeed. I wonder about the rest of the evening. What will Laurette do? Will she try to seduce me to make her husband's job easier? Well, I'm not against it, I still have the memory of her lips on my little cock....

George puts down his cup and goes to stand behind Francine, his hands on her shoulders. He remains motionless, the cup suspended. His hands slide down her blouse, to the bulge in her chest. My wife stares at me, wide-eyed. She doesn't react when

Laurette removes her cup. I smile and blow her a kiss with my fingertips. She sighs and lets go against the back of the couch, accepting her defeat. George makes no mistake, he caresses my wife's breasts with his hands and kisses her on the neck. Our defeat I should say because Laurette comes to join me in my armchair and stretches her lips for a kiss that I do not refuse her....

Georges pounds Francine with his kidneys on the couch while, with his thighs on my shoulders, I brush against Laurette's pussy, which makes little meows every time I bite her clit. As for me, it's been a long time since I've put my offering between the doctor's fingers, ever since the first strokes. Francine's moans of pleasure keep me going and I try to satisfy my partner. Fingers, tongue, teeth, I use everything so that she receives as much pleasure as my wife shows. Ouch! Laurette pulls my hair. No matter, it's a sign that my efforts are achieving their goal. I insist, she lets out a loud, almost screaming moan and collapses against the back of the chair. On the couch, Georges and Francine, still clinging to each other, struggle to breathe normally.

Laurette pushes me away. She gets up, pulls my wife out of her husband's arms and leads her to the bathroom. George gets rid of the pants and underwear that were cluttering one leg.

- I think we'd better get completely undressed," he says, taking off his shirt.

So it's not over yet? Why not? I finish undressing and it's two naked men receiving their wives back from the bathroom, a glass of cognac in hand. I am dazzled by the sight of them appearing in Eva's clothes. How beautiful they look!

Francine is also relieved to see us naked. I guess Laurette insisted that she take off her last few clothes. She sits next to me on the couch, one hand gently on my sex. I kiss her near the ear.

- She made you come, George, didn't she?

- Are you angry with me?

- Not at all, my dear. I'm happy for this pleasure I can no longer give you.

- It's you I love.

- I know that and I thank you for it.

George hands her a glass of liquor.

- Here, drink this, it will do you good.

Francine lowers her lips.

- Oh, how nice! What is it?

- Yellow Chartreuse. I'm glad you like it.

- Come sit next to me," Laurette asks and sets down her glass.

Francine looks at me, I give her permission with a twinkle in my eye. Her friend pulls her between her thighs and caresses her breasts, whose nipples point, betraying my wife's excitement. Laurette bends her over and their lips meet.

George sits down next to me. I feel the tickle of hair on his thighs.

- Aren't you surprised?" he asks me.

- No, I suspected your wife was attracted to mine.

- Yes, she is bisexual.

Bi? Oh yes, she is! Bisexual, in love with both men and women.

- Um... Me too," she admits in a whisper.

Caught up in the spectacle of the two women, I don't get up. His hand slides up my thigh and fiddles with my wrinkled sex. It feels as good as it does with female fingers. Suddenly I realize what she's told me: it's my ass she wants! No, not that one! I'm not attracted to men! And it's not the rape I suffered three months ago that has changed my mind. I move back to the corner of the couch. He stares at me unhappily. Oh, that look! It brings back from the depths of my memory an episode I thought I had forgotten. I think back to many years ago to a study at the university; a friend, after an exhausting revision together, had looked at me with the same look of a whipped dog.... I hadn't been able to resist... An experience with no future, despite the pleasure I had discovered.

George slides toward me, his eyes pleading. I watch him advance, unable to react. What is happening to me? The same inertia had paralyzed me when my boyfriend had opened my jeans. The memory of the pleasure I had felt in those distant moments rises to the surface. I suddenly regret that my torturers had been so brutal.... My friend will surely hurt me less.... What am I saying here? I'm not turning gay after all!.... I realize at this moment that my first and distant foray into the homosexual universe has remained unique not because of conviction but rather because of lack of opportunity, fear of what people will say, cowardice perhaps...

The hand finds my thigh and slowly moves up to my groin. The skin is covered in goose bumps. I am overwhelmed by the obvious: I burn to find the sensations buried deep in my subconscious that the brutality of my torturers had failed to exhume. I am convinced that Georges will make me rediscover them. To silence the suspicion of shame that persists when I abandon myself, I convince myself that I owe it to him. I am grateful to him for the pleasure he has given my wife and I would be remiss to refuse him the reward he hopes for....

In a sign of agreement, I place my hand on his cock, which stiffens between my fingers. I let out a heavy sigh: to think that a few months ago -an eternity- I was carrying such a triumphant scepter. Finally, the past is past, let's enjoy the present without complexes! Georges turns me on my stomach against the arm of the sofa. In the armchair opposite me, Francine receives Laurette's oral caresses between her legs. We smile at each other, amused by the symmetry of our relationship with our friends.

I was right not to worry. Georges is very considerate, the introduction, well prepared by the caresses, goes smoothly. The friction in the sphincter sends only beneficial waves through my body. No pain comes to spoil my pleasure.... Yes! My friend who guesses my desires passes his arm under my belly and rolls my sex between his fingers. In the armchair, Laurette has managed to go head-to-head with Francine. I catch her gaze. I can see the recognition in it. Yes, we are happy with our partner's happiness. Pleasure invades me, rises in the shaft that I feel, to my delight, growing.

- I... I'm going to come.

- Good," George replies.

- But... the sofa.

- No problem...the skin...washes away.

He doubles his loins. I lay back on his palm, a little disappointed because I wish I could have resisted as much as he did. That doesn't stop me from shuddering with happiness as his cum rises and distorts my gut. Then the cock deflates, slides out and escapes, leaving me to regret its size in my ass. In the armchair, the two women don't stop making each other cum....

Later in the night, on the big bed where all four of us will be, Georges and Laurette make love while Francine and I cover them with our caresses before falling asleep, overcome by fatigue, a healthy and sweet fatigue...

Tonight, or rather tonight, was the first in a series that continues. At first Francine was angry at the pleasure Georges was giving her. Laurette knew better than I how to reassure her that our two couples were not in danger. She and her husband confessed that they had long dreamed of transforming the friendship that bound us into a more intimate relationship but did not dare in the face of our apparent indifference. I remember the discreet calls and suggestions they made to us, but at the time neither Francine nor I, as selfish and fulfilled lovers, were able to understand them. It was only after the revelation of my problems and the ease with which, first I and then Francine, accepted Laurette's caresses that she began to hope. I now understand her disappointment when she learned that we had not been protected during our rape: she had to wait another two months!

We spend most weekends together, both at our house and at their house. We have instituted a rotation. Every time we meet, one of the four of us is greeted by the other three. I have become a specialist in all types of petting and can make people forget that they are no longer able to penetrate.

Francine and I talked a lot about our misadventure, especially in the two months leading up to the relationship change with Laurette and her husband. She agreed that the first part of the evening had gone well and that if I didn't accept Joseph's invitation she would remember it well. I often think back and remember with excitement the pleasure I felt when she masturbated while Joseph fucked her.

I waited for Francine to admit without remorse that we were playing square with our friends before suggesting that we go back to the club. It wasn't easy, but she was finally convinced when I vowed that I would never accept another invitation to go out. The first night, when I rang the doorbell, I told her that after the first successful hug with Joseph, I had imagined doing it again, but this time completely naked. She screams, but her indignation rings hollow because she doesn't demand to leave. She blushes when I look at her mockingly and presses the doorbell herself. My former colleague greets us warmly. Having learned of our difficulties with Joseph, he assures me that he will introduce us to a friend we can trust. This friend does not disappoint us.

He doesn't care about Francine's reticence and takes us to a private room where my wife agrees to let us undress her. I rediscover with pleasure the sensations I had discovered the first time, amplified by the contact of our skin, and I am sure Francine feels the same.

We are now regulars at the club where we go about once a month. We are called the Inseparables because both she and I refuse to hug outside the presence of our spouse. Our partners quickly realized that while the state of my genitals did not allow me to honor people of the so-called weaker sex, I was not averse to receiving male tributes. Most of the time we are penetrated simultaneously while face to face we kiss and his hand masturbates my cock that is never as big as in these moments.

No, I don't regret what happened to me, what some would call a handicap. I would rather say I was lucky. The ordeal has brought us together as a couple and we live a fulfilling life. During the day, I work as a volunteer for a rehabilitation organization and in the evenings Francine and I share tender moments in bed. She assures me that weekends with Laurette and Georges and evenings at the club are enough to satisfy the sexual needs I can't fulfill.

I look at the clock. It's getting late. Francine will be home from work soon and Laurette and Georges will be back soon. Tonight it is my turn to receive their caresses. I know the two women will fight for my little cock. I love it when their mouths close on my sex but I prefer Francine who alone knows how to roll the glans between her tongue and palate. Ah, to be sucked by her while Georges inserts his cock into my ass.... Foot!